Stories of Dragons

Christopher Rawson
Adapted by Lesley Sims

Illustrated by
Stephen Cartwright

Reading Consultant: Alison Kelly
Roehampton University

Contents

Chapter 1

All about dragons

Years ago, dragons were the terror of towns... or so it was said. They breathed in air and blew out flame. Just one puff of dragon breath could kill you.

Some dragons lived in caves, guarding stolen treasure.

Others lived under the sea. Sometimes, they popped up and scared sailors.

Dragons even lived in the sky. When they were angry, storms blew up.

Bolts of lightning were flames shot from a cross dragon's nose.

Most people kept as far away from dragons as they could. Only knights dared go near them.

People offered huge rewards to the brave knights who could kill dragons. But dragons weren't so easy to defeat.

Dragons had bumpy scales, flapping wings and pointed tails, and they came in all shapes and sizes.

Whatever they looked like, you wouldn't want to meet one.

Chapter 2

Stan and the dragon

Stan was a woodcutter. He lived deep in the forest with his wife. She was sad because they had no children.

One day, a wizard appeared in the forest. "You're a good man, Stan," said the wizard. "I can grant you one wish."

Stan only wanted one wish.

"I wish for as many children as my wife is thinking about now," he said.

Stan's wish came true! But they didn't have two... or ten... or even fifty children. They had one hundred.

"How will I afford to feed them all?" said Stan.

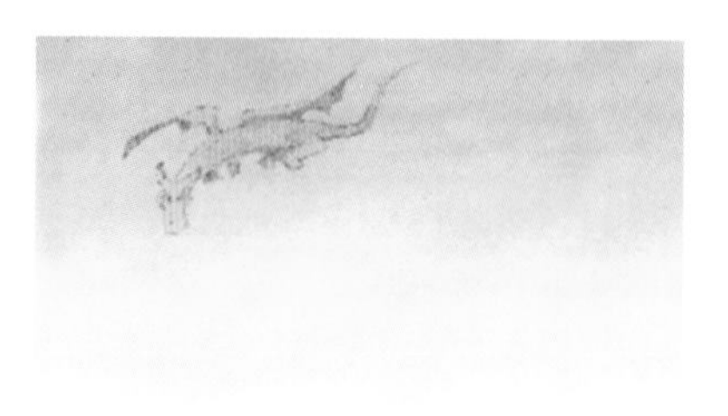

His friend Sam had an idea.

"A dragon has been scaring my sheep," he said. "If you can find its cave, you might find treasure."

So, Stan set off in search of the dragon and its treasure.

Stan didn't find the dragon. The dragon found him. When he saw it, Stan knew he couldn't fight the dragon.

Instead, he said, "I bet I'm stronger than you. I can squeeze a stone until it drips!"

"You are strong!" grunted the dragon. He didn't know Stan's stone was a lump of old cheese.

The dragon took Stan to meet his mother.

"It must have been a trick," she said. "If you really are stronger than my son, I'll give you our treasure."

She found two clubs. "See how far you can both throw these."

"I'll throw mine over that mountain," said the dragon. "How about you?"

"I can't throw now," Stan said. "The moon's in the way!"

Now, the dragons were scared. Stan was the strongest man they had ever met. They made a plan to kill him in the night.

But Stan heard them. He decided to fool them and put a log in his bed.

In the middle of the night, the dragon crept to Stan's bed.

BAM! He whacked the bed just where he thought Stan's head was.

"That's killed him!" said the dragon.

When Stan appeared next morning, the dragons were astonished.

"I have a little bump on my head," he said. "Perhaps a flea bit me in the night?"

Stan was much too clever for the terrified dragons. They took out their treasure.

"Here," they said. "Take it! Just go away and leave us alone!"

They even carried the treasure home for him. Stan had enough gold to buy his huge family all the food they could eat.

Chapter 3

The wicked worm

Tom loved fishing... until the afternoon he caught a worm instead of a fish.

An old man had seen him.

"That worm is trouble," he warned Tom. "But don't throw it back in the river. You'll only make things worse."

Tom didn't know what to do. He tried to hide the worm in a well.

But a week later, the worm crawled out. It had grown even bigger.

The worm was hungry and angry. It chased the cows around the fields. Then it chased the villagers around their houses.

Tom felt terrible. The worm was a menace – and it was all his fault.

Brave knights came from miles around to kill the worm. But it was too strong.

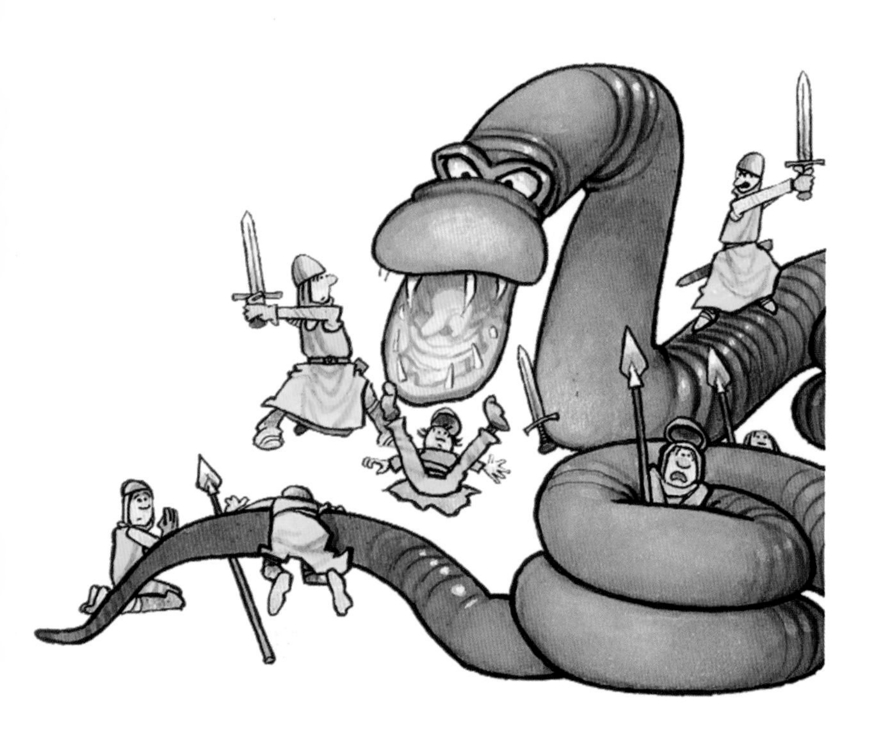

It curled itself around them and squeezed them so they couldn't fight.

Finally, Tom went to see a wise woman to ask for help.

"You caught it. You must get rid of it," she told Tom.

Tom wasn't sure about that. The dragon had never hurt anyone... because everyone left him alone.

But Tom had no choice. So, he dressed up like a brave knight and went to beg the dragon for help.

To his surprise, the dragon didn't look scary at all.

"What's wrong?" said Tom.

"I'm lonely," the dragon replied. "I have no friends."

"I know how you can have a hundred!" Tom told him. "But you'll have to look fierce."

Tom told the dragon about the worm. “If you eat the worm, everyone in the village will be your friend!” he said.

“I can’t eat it,” said the dragon. “I’m a vegetarian.”

It was so hot, the worm was swimming. The dragon stood on the river bank, opened his mouth and roared. "Yum!" he cried. "Supper!"

The worm took one look at the dragon and swam for its life. It was never seen again.

Chapter 4

Victor saves the village

Victor made barrels, the best barrels in the country.

He made the best barrels because he used the best wood. He hunted hard to find the tallest, straightest trees.

He was always looking out for the perfect tree. So he didn't always watch where he was going. One day, he tripped and fell...

...into a cave.

Try as he might...

...Victor couldn't climb out of the cave.

Suddenly, he heard a deep growl. There was something behind him! Victor looked. He wished he hadn't.

“Please don’t eat me!” Victor begged.

“We won’t,” said one of the dragons. “Not yet. We’re going to sleep. Wake us up in the spring.”

Victor was stuck. Soon, he was bored as well.

There was nothing he could do.

He had to wait until spring.

All he had to eat and drink were grass and water. After a while, he was no longer as round as a barrel. He was as thin as a twig.

Finally, the dragons awoke.

"We can't eat you!" said one. "You're skin and bone."

"Grab my tail," the other dragon said to Victor. "We'll take you home. Perhaps your friends will make a juicy meal."

The villagers were amazed to see Victor after so long, and they were terrified to see the dragons.

But before the dragons could bite anyone, Victor invited them to a huge feast.

Victor and the dragons ate for a week. The dragons enjoyed the food so much, they decided they would never eat people again.

The villagers were very pleased to hear it. They put up a statue of Victor in the market square.

Now, everyone who visits knows how Victor saved the village from two hungry dragons.

Try these other books in
Series One:

The Burglar's Breakfast: Alfie Briggs is a burglar, who discovers someone has stolen his breakfast!

The Dinosaurs Next Door: Mr. Puff's house is full of amazing things. Best of all are the dinosaur eggs – until they begin to hatch...

Wizards: One wizard looks after orphans, one sells cures and one must stop a band of robbers from taking the last sack of gold in the castle.

The Monster Gang: The Monster Gang is together for their first meeting in the tree house. But one of the monsters hides a secret.

Designed by
Katarina Dragoslavić

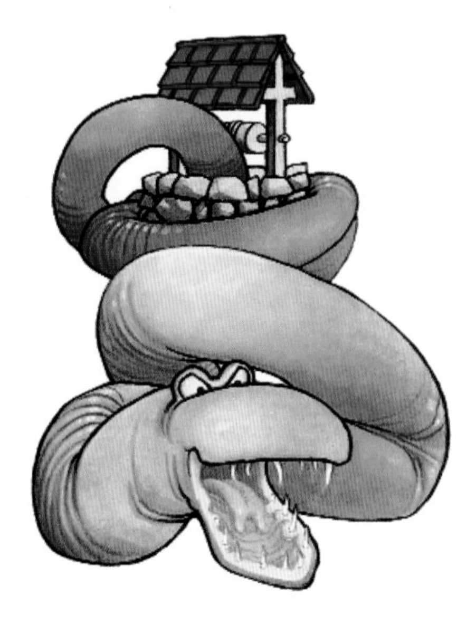

This edition first published in 2007 by Usborne Publishing Ltd.,
Usborne House, 83-85 Saffron Hill, London EC1N 8RT, England.
www.usborne.com

Printed in China. UE. First published in America in 2004.